Favorite CHRISTMAS Carols

illustrated by PAT PARIS

The Standard Publishing Company, Cincinnati, Ohio. A division of Standex International Corporation.
© 1999 by The Standard Publishing Company.
Bean Sprouts™ and the Bean Sprouts design logo are trademarks of Standard Publishing.
Printed in the United States of America. All rights reserved.
Music typesetting by John Morton. Cover design by Robert Glover.

06 05 04 03 02 01 00 99   5 4 3 2 1

ISBN 0-7847-1085-6

Standard
Publishing
Cincinnati, Ohio

Deck the Halls

Traditional Welsh Melody

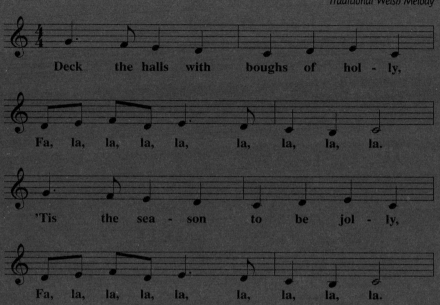

Deck   the halls   with   boughs   of   hol - ly,

Fa,   la,   la,   la,   la,   la,   la,   la,   la.

'Tis   the   sea - son   to   be   jol - ly,

Fa,   la,   la,   la,   la,   la,   la,   la,   la.

O Little Town of Bethlehem

Phillips Brooks

Lewis H. Redner

O lit - tle town of Beth - le - hem, how
still we__ see thee lie! A - bove thy deep and
dream - less sleep the si - lent__ stars go by.
Yet in thy dark streets shin - eth the
ev - er - last - ing Light; The hopes and fears of
all the years are met in thee to - night.

Away in a Manger

Martin Luther
James R. Murray

A - way   in a   man - ger,   no

crib   for   a   bed,   the   lit - tle Lord

Je - sus laid   down his sweet head. The

stars in the sky___ looked down where he

lay,   the   lit - tle Lord   Je - sus,   a -

sleep   on   the   hay.

Hark! The Herald Angels Sing

Charles Wesley

Felix Mendelssohn

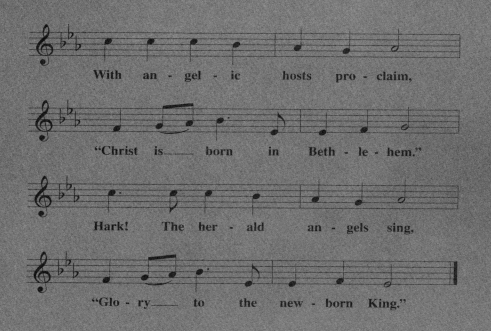

With an - gel - ic hosts pro - claim,

"Christ is— born in Beth - le - hem."

Hark! The her - ald an - gels sing,

"Glo - ry— to the new - born King."

What Child Is This?

William C. Dix

Traditional English Melody, "Greensleeves"

What Child is this, — who, laid to rest, — on

Ma-ry's lap — is sleep-ing? Whom an-gels greet — with

an-thems sweet, — while shep-herds watch — are

keep-ing? This, this — is Christ the King, — whom

shep-herds guard — and an-gels sing:

Haste, haste — to bring him laud, — the

Babe, — the Son — of Ma - ry.

Go, Tell It on the Mountain

Traditional Spiritual

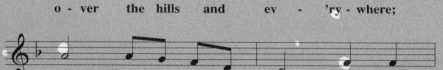

Go, tell it on the moun - tain,

o - ver the hills and ev - 'ry - where;

Go, tell it on the moun - tain that

Fine

Je - sus Christ____ is born.

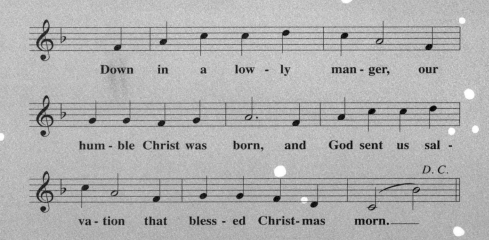

Down in a low - ly man - ger, our hum - ble Christ was born, and God sent us sal - va - tion that bless - ed Christ - mas morn._____

D.C.

We Three Kings of Orient Are

John Hopkins   *John Hopkins*

O Come, All Ye Faithful

Trans. by Frederick Oakeley

Latin Hymn

O come, all ye faith-ful, joy-ful and tri-um-phant. O come ye, O come ye to Beth-le-hem. Come and be-hold him, born the King of an-gels. O come, let us a-dore him! O come, let us a-dore him! O come, let us a-dore him, Christ, the Lord!

Angels We Have Heard on High

Traditional

Old French Carol

An - gels we have heard on high,

sweet - ly sing - ing o'er the plains.

And the moun - tains in re - ply,

e - cho - ing their joy - ous strains:

Glo - ri - a in ex - cel - sis De - o!

Glo - ri - a in ex - cel - sis De - o!

Silent Night

Joseph Mohr

Franz Gruber

We Wish You a Merry Christmas

Traditional English Melody